W9-CPZ-741

Lena Landström

WILL'S NEW CAP

Translated by Richard E. Fisher

R&S
BOOKS

Stockholm   New York   London   Adelaide   Toronto

Rabén & Sjögren Stockholm
Translation copyright © 1992 by Richard E. Fisher
All rights reserved
Originally published in Sweden by Rabén & Sjögren
under the title *Nisses nya mössa*, pictures and text copyright © 1990
by Olof and Lena Landström
Library of Congress catalog card number: 91-42407
Printed in Denmark
First edition, 1992
Second printing, 1993

ISBN 91 29 62062 7

Will gets a new cap with a visor.

He goes outside right away.

John, Peter, Karen, and Susan are playing in the yard.

They all want to try on Will's new cap.

Mama asks Will to buy a newspaper.

The sun is shining — but not in Will's eyes.
A visor is really practical.

And good looking!

Will buys the newspaper.

Now it's raining!

No problem. The visor protects him.

Now it's pouring!
Will tucks the paper under his sweater
and runs.

The visor begins to wilt.
Will can't see.

Ouch!

Blood!

Will limps all the way home.

Now he can cry.

He gets a bandage on his knee,
and a soda.

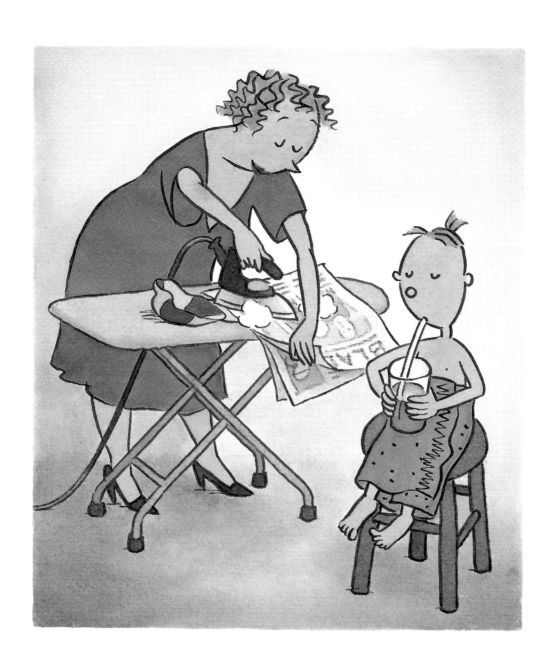

Mama irons the visor dry.

But what now?

Something has happened.

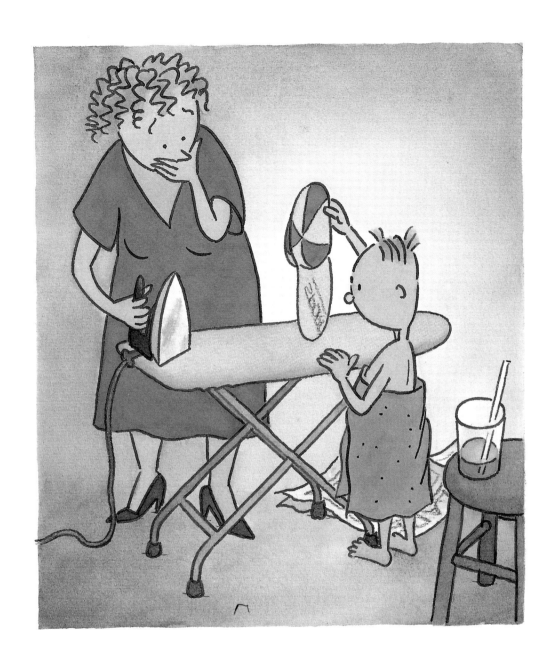

The newspaper print has stuck to the visor.

Has Will's new cap been ruined?

Not at all. It's as good as new.

It fits almost better than before.